HANSEL AND GRETA

Jeanette Winterson

WITH ILLUSTRATIONS BY

Laura Barrett

HaymarketBooks
Chicago, Illinois

Deep in the woods.
Deep in the woods.
Deep in the woods.
Are we there yet?
Not yet.

Here's my brother, Hansel. Not very tall but really cool. He knows how to talk to trees.

Here's my dad. He's a lumberjack who works in the forest behind our house.

Here's GreedyGuts. Our mum's big sister. Our mum's REALLY big sister. She's at least ten feet tall and five feet wide. She eats all day: YumYumYum. She sleeps all night: SnoreSnoreSnore. She eats things you would never, ever eat. Once she was so hungry at breakfast time that she ate the toaster as well as the toast. Secretly I think GreedyGuts is an ogre, but Dad says it's rude to think like that about your auntie.

My name is Greta.

"GRETA! Toast me a family-size loaf of bread. Spread it with a pound of butter and six jars of strawberry jam." That's breakfast.

"GRETA! Make me forty pancakes with a bucket of maple syrup." That's lunch.

"GRETA! I want ten sausages with eighty-five oven fries and 240 peas." That's dinner.

GreedyGuts came to live with us when our mother died. We had never seen her before, so our mom can't have liked her very much. Dad was worried about going out to work as well as looking after us. But really, we look after him.

My dad works in the forest. He's cutting down trees because there's a big railway line coming through the forest. There's already a small railway line, and sometimes we go and wave at the trains. This new one will have high fences and go too fast for waving.

One day Dad came home from work. He was sad.

"Greta, I don't want to cut down any more trees. What about the birds? What about the animals? The forest is a home. Today there was a white dove in a birch tree, and she cried out *Home Home Home!* I didn't cut down the tree, but if my boss finds out he'll fire me."

Dad's boss is horrible. He only cares about money. He has a big black beard all over his face. All you can see are his red nose and beady eyes. The rest is beard. I call him BeardFace.

Dad worries a lot. He worries about me and Hansel, and now he's worried about the forest. I hugged him and made him some hot chocolate while I was trying to think of a good idea.

"Dad! We can start planting trees in the forest. Then the forest will grow again, and the birds and the animals will have somewhere to live."

"But how are we going to plant trees?" said Dad. "We don't have any trees."

Hansel was listening. He said, "Trees have trees! We can get acorns from the oak trees and chestnuts from the chestnut trees and beech nuts from the beech trees and apple pips from the apple trees, and we can plant them in pots until they are big enough to go outside and grow on their own."

Dad was happy, and we started our adventure together. It wasn't a speedy adventure like you see in cartoons. We found out that it takes a lot of time to grow something. It takes a lot more time for anything to grow than it does for anything to be chopped down.

GreedyGuts found out what we were doing.

"What a waste of time! You're just like that stupid Swedish child, Greta Iceberg."

"Her name is Greta Thunberg," I said.

"Somebody should go to Sweden and eat her," said GreedyGuts. "'I'll have a Greta Tonburger. With chips.' Hahahahahaha. Now fry me some onions, you stupid girl."

I'm not stupid, I said, but I said it in my head, so that she wouldn't wallop me with her giant hand the size of a pizza shovel.

GreedyGuts plonked herself down at the table and started eating the socks I had just brought in from the washing line. She likes blue socks best.

"There'll be dinner soon," I said. "Shepherd's pie."

"There's never any shepherd in it though, is there?" said GreedyGuts. "Why don't you cook properly, you horrible little vegetarian?"

"It's not nice to eat people," I said.

Next day there was good news! GreedyGuts is going on a trip to stay with her best friend, GuzzleGuts. GuzzleGuts lives in the city.

We helped her pack her twenty-five suitcases onto the bus. We waved and waved until the bus was nothing but an exhaust cloud in the distance.

"Phew!" said Hansel. "She's gone."

So now it's Hansel, Hansel's pet blackbird, Chirp, me, my pet cat, Snatcher, Dad. Now GreedyGuts is gone, things are much better.

Autumn came. Deep in the wood we gathered all the nuts and seeds and acorns we wanted to plant.

Winter came. The land was covered in snow.

Spring came. The sun shone. Hansel, Dad, Chirp, Snatcher, and I went into the woods to start planting our little trees.

"Listen!" said Hansel. "The trees are saying thank you!" But

I could only hear the wind in the leaves and the creak of the branches.

"Put your arms around this birch tree," said Hansel. "Put your ear close up against the bark and listen."

I put my arms around the tree, and I remembered how our mother used to put her arms around us and how she was as big as a tree to us when we were small and how she was like the canopy of this forest—sheltering, loving, watching over us. Home.

"Are you OK, Greta?" asked Dad.

"Trees are alive like we are alive, aren't they, Dad?"

"Yes, Greta. Everything is life."

At night Dad was reading to us from *Treasure Island* by Robert Louis Stevenson. Jim Hawkins is just a kid, but he saves the day and wins the treasure.

"Do you think we can save the day and win the treasure?" I asked Hansel, when we were tucked up in our little beds.

"First you have to believe that the treasure is really there," said Hansel.

One day Dad was in the forest on his own. It was early morning. The sun fell in golden pieces through the canopy of trees so that the forest floor looked like a jigsaw puzzle made of gold. The birds that flew through the sunlight were golden birds. Dad saw a colony of wild honeybees wearing their golden coats.

"This is treasure," he said to himself. "This is all the treasure in the world."

BeardFace the Boss was nearby. He saw Dad standing with his head back, looking at the beautiful world.

"What's got into you?"

"We should be protecting this forest, not destroying it," said Dad. "I can't do this anymore."

So Dad came home. He put down his chainsaw and his axe.

He took off his steel-toed boots and heavy jacket. He hung up his safety helmet, washed his hands, and sat staring into the fire. "I've lost my job," he said. "Now what?"

We were proud of our dad for standing up to BeardFace. We hugged him and told him not to worry.

"Worry or not," said Dad, "we've still got to eat."

"I've got an idea!" said Hansel. "We can plant for the forest but we can plant for ourselves too. Let's start a vegetable garden at home."

"That's a great idea," said Dad. "We know how to grow from seeds now."

"And we won't have to buy vegetables in plastic bags," I said. "And maybe I can learn how to bake bread."

"I'll go shopping on my bike," said Hansel. "Then we don't have to use the car."

"We can save lots of money," I said. We planted potatoes in trenches and carrots in rows and cabbages in squares and green beans on sticks and spinach in long lines and raspberries on wires and great big orange pumpkins to grin at us when autumn came.

I had six hens to lay eggs, and Hansel learned how to catch fish in the stream. If a fish was too small he put it back.

Dad wasn't sad anymore.
Everything was going well.
Then GreedyGuts came home.

The taxi driver struggled to get her twenty-five suitcases out of the car. GreedyGuts sat in the back finishing off a family-size bag of sour cream 'n' onion chips. Finally she got out.

"FOOD!" she shouted. "FOOD FOOD FOOD NOW NOW NOW." I gave her a bowl of homegrown leek and potato soup with homemade bread. GreedyGuts took one mouthful and spat it out all over the cat. "FOOD, MY NOSE! This isn't food! I WANT

PIZZA AND CHIPS."

"I can make you a cheese sandwich," I said.

"I WANT SALTED CARAMEL ICE CREAM! NOW!"

Dad explained to GreedyGuts that we were trying to live in harmony with Nature—not eat too much, not make too much waste, grow our own food. GreedyGuts was red-faced with rage. Her big round head looked like a monster tomato.

Hansel was sitting at the table doing a jigsaw puzzle of London. GreedyGuts grabbed a handful of the cardboard pieces and stuffed them into her mouth.

"Hey! That's Buckingham Palace you're eating!" shouted Hansel.

"WAIT TILL I TELL GUZZLEGUTS HOW YOU TREAT ME!"

GreedyGuts yackety-yacked down the phone to GuzzleGuts, and the next day a huge pizza oven was delivered. Dad had to install it for her and make her a load of charcoal. When we fired it up it looked like a big red mouth. Actually, it looked like GreedyGuts's mouth.

For about six weeks GreedyGuts was happy, eating twenty-nine inflatable pizzas every day.

Then she was unhappy because she had no money left and she couldn't buy even one frozen deflated pizza. That's when Dad discovered that GreedyGuts had hacked into his bank account and spent all his money on pizzas, lemonade, chocolate-flavored dresses, and handbags.

"How am I going to pay the bills?" said Dad.

"You'll have to get a job, won't you?" said GreedyGuts.

"Maybe you should get a job," said Dad, and then GreedyGuts exploded into a human mushroom cloud like a badly treated atomic bomb and screamed about how all she did was look after our good-for-nothing family in memory of her saintly sister (aka our mother), now dead, and probably our fault. She turned on my father, waving her big fists in his face.

"Send these stupid children out to work. There must be some chimneys they can clean! Why don't they join the army and send us their pay?"

"I'm twelve!" I said. "I'm too big to go up chimneys and too small to join the army."

"Excuses! Excuses!" shouted GreedyGuts. "What about him? That boy, Herman."

"My name is Hansel," said Hansel. "I could go up a chimney, in theory, but nobody has a coal fire anymore. Coal is very bad for the planet."

"Planet, my nose!" yelled GreedyGuts. "The point of life is to eat as much as possible, make as much money as possible, go on vacation as much as possible, have as many clothes as possible, buy thousands of household appliances, two new cars every year, a Jacuzzi in the yard, and a Luxury-Level Executive Home. Not oats, lettuce, and a bicycle."

"You could always leave," I said, because I am optimistic by nature.

GreedyGuts jabbed her fingers in my face. It was like being attacked by ten angry sausages.

"Since I came back here, in loving memory of my dear, departed sister, to do my duty by her family, and after eating nothing but rabbit food and a few inflatable pizzas, I have lost at least four ounces. That is a quarter pound of myself! My actual self!"

"You have also eaten the fridge," I said.

"The door wouldn't open," wept GreedyGuts. "The only way

I could get at the food was by eating the entire fridge. All that metal. So hard. I broke a tooth."

Absently, she picked up the tin opener and chewed it to bits while she shed molten tears.

Poor Dad. He hates it when anybody cries. He said, "Children! I'll get a job in the city and earn some money for us. GreedyGuts will take care of you while I'm gone."

"No, she won't!" I said. "She'll eat us!"

"Of course she won't eat you!" said Dad.

She didn't eat us.

First she ate my chickens so that we didn't have any eggs. Then she made Hansel fish all the fish out of the stream so that no fish were left.

Then one day, while I was watering the spinach, Hansel came running up; his face was streaked with tears, and he was holding a black feather. "She's eaten Chirp!"

I dropped my watering can and ran into the kitchen. GreedyGuts was sitting at the kitchen table with an identical black feather sticking out of her over-stocked mouth. In between her ox-sized fists was a super-size burger bun. Inside the burger bun was a pan-fried blackbird.

"You are eating Hansel's friend!" I said.

"Friend, my nose!" said GreedyGuts. "If you want to make friends, don't make friends with anything that can be eaten!"

Poor Hansel was shaking with sadness. I took him upstairs to our little bedroom.

"She'll eat the cat next," I said, looking at Snatcher, walking on the wall outside.

"We should run away," said Hansel.

But before we could run away, GreedyGuts made a plan of her own.

The next morning, before it was even light, I heard a truck revving up.

I looked through the window, and there was Dad's horrible ex-boss, BeardFace, from the logging company.

"Dear children!" said GreedyGuts, as Hansel and I came downstairs. "My wonderful, precious Gretawig and Handlebars, as a special treat I am sending you away to play in the lovely forest for a whole day. Mr. Munroe here will take you."

"No problem!" said BeardFace. "I love children."

"Oh, me too," said GreedyGuts. "Here's a sandwich each. Goodbye."

As we shot down the road, Snatcher jumped in over the tailgate. At least we were together.

"Where are we going?" I said.

"Deep in the woods," BeardFace replied.

What he didn't notice was that Hansel had a pocketful of colored marbles and was throwing them out of the window one by one by one.

"End of the line!" said BeardFace.

We had never been to this part of the woods before. The trees were charred and burned. Dead and decayed branches littered the muddy floor. There was an abandoned hut with a tin roof.

"You like planting trees, don't you? Plenty of room here!" BeardFace reached into the front passenger seat and pulled out trays of our little seeds in little pots.

"Wait!" I said. "Be careful!"

"OK!" said BeardFace. "Gotta rush. Have a nice life!" With that, he jumped into the truck and went back down the bumpy forest track.

"GreedyGuts wants to kill us," I said to Hansel.

"Yep. But we're going right back home to kill her. Or something," said Hansel. "It's our house! All we have to do is follow the marbles."

"What is this place?" I said as we looked around. "This desolate place?"

There was nothing alive. Not a bird, not a fox, not a squirrel, not a blade of grass. A few burned-out trees shivered sadly in the wind.

"This must be where they chopped everything down," Hansel said. "No forest left."

"But look!" I said. "Someone lived here once."

It was true. There was a blue door lying in a heap of rubble, and still struggling to grow by the door was a little apple tree with two branches.

"Let's go," I said. "This place gives me the creeps."

"No, wait," said Hansel. "The tree is talking to me."

Hansel went over to the tree and put his hand on its bark. Suddenly the tree jumped forward like a pogo stick.

"Greetings and salutations!" said the Little Tree.

"Trees don't talk!" I said.

"Yes, they do," said Hansel.

"I thought you talked to them! I didn't think they talked to you!"

Hansel shrugged. The Little Tree said, "It is a matter of listening."

"Is this your house?" said Hansel.

"My friend the Witch in the Wood used to live here," said

the Little Tree. "The bulldozers frightened her away. Will you help me to find her?"

I looked at Hansel. "First we need to go home and call our dad. He'll know where your friend has gone."

"Well, then," said the Little Tree. "Lead on."

"Trees don't walk," I said.

"These are difficult times," said the Little Tree. "One must do what one must do." And the tree gave a jump and then another jump. Then the Little Tree fell over and Hansel picked it up.

"Practice makes perfect," said the Little Tree. "First time for everything!"

"OK," said Hansel. "Let's go."

We walked and we walked and we walked. There's a marble! Where's a marble? And another! And another!

It was tiring for us, but the Little Tree was exhausted. Finally, the poor thing just fell over like it was dead.

"I don't know how you children do it all day—walk, I mean. Much nicer to stay in one place and let one's friends come to you. It used to be a beautiful place where we lived. The witch was so kind."

"Witches are mean and nasty," I said.

"Some are mean and nasty," said the Little Tree. "But that is true of everyone, rich and poor, boy or girl. Animals too. I once met a very nasty rabbit. Nibbled my bark."

"We can plant you at our house if you like," I said. "We've got a little orchard."

"Oh, I should love that," said the Little Tree. "But first we must find my friend."

"And we've got to find our dad," said Hansel. "Come on!"

And we did go on. And on. And on.

And then it started to rain.

The rain made so much mud that we couldn't find a single marble anymore. We were filthy, battered, soaked, lost. Alone.

"There's an oak tree," said Hansel. "She'll shelter us." We ran underneath the big, wide, dense branches. It was dry underneath there. I held Hansel's hand.

"Listen!" said Hansel. "The trees are talking to each other. They are wondering why we are here."

Hansel jumped up. "Help us!" he shouted, looking into the wild and windy top of the great oak. "We are small and you are big. We are young and you are wise. Help us!"

There was a sound like thunder, deep and low and rumbling. "Who calls me?" said the Oak Tree.

"It's me! Hansel! Here's my sister, Greta. Here's our cat, Snatcher. Here's our new friend, who is also a tree."

16

"A walking tree?" said the Oak Tree.

"Temporarily," said the Little Tree, a bit embarrassed to be so undignified. "Very tiring it is, too."

"We are the children planting a new forest!" shouted Hansel. "Today we are lost."

And then something strange started to happen. There was a rumbling tumbling grumbling zumbling jumbling (not bumbling or mumbling or pumbling) sound, like a lot of things happening at once.

Then a branch flew off the Oak Tree and landed in front of us—splat. Then another and another—in lines like signs pointing the way.

"Come on!" said Hansel. "Follow the trees."

Wet through, and shivering with cold, we came at last to a river. Willow trees stood on either side.

"Help us!" shouted Hansel. But the willow trees only rustled among themselves.

"Wait!" said the Little Tree. "Willows are very shy. But I can see my cousin the Crab Apple over there!"

The Little Tree hopped through the wind and rain to a short, gnarly, moss-covered old tree. Their leaves mingled into each other, like heads together.

Slowly, slowly, the rustling willows on either side of the bank began to bend down in slow motion. Slowly they bent their backs and made a bendy bridge for us to cross. The bridge was moving. The bridge was alive.

We crossed the rushing river on the backs of the willow trees.

"After this," said Hansel, "we can follow the silver birches that shine so bright in the moonlight, and they will lead us home."

And so we made our way out of the forest.

BANGA BANGA TWANGA TWANGA TWINGA TWONGA, PING PINGY PING PING BOOM BOOM!

As we approached our house we could see that lots of people were having a party. There was a big tent with people dancing, and there were lanterns and music, the pizza oven was roaring-red, and, worst of all, there was GreedyGuts dancing with BeardFace.

"Let's sneak around the back," Hansel said.

No one was expecting us, so it was easy to dodge around and climb in through the kitchen window.

Then we crept into our bedroom. But it wasn't our bedroom anymore! Someone else's clothes were all over the floor. Someone else's dressing gown was hanging behind the door. Someone else's head was on my pillow.

The head woke up. "Who the dog's chopsticks are you?"

"We're Hansel and Greta. We live here."

"Oh, no, you don't, you little liars! GorgeousGuts lives here!" Then he jumped out of bed in his Superman pajamas and started yelling out of the window. "Hey! There's two ugly skinny muddy wet runaway ragbag kids in MY bedroom!"

The music stopped. TWANG TWING TWOY–NG. There was a terrible scream of rage and disbelief, and then five thousand Doritos splattered against the window from GreedyGuts's open mouth.

We ran as fast as we could, but a giant of a man, sweating like a sizzling sausage, caught us by our shoulders and carried us outside. This turned out to be BeardFace's brother: BogFace. He dropped us

on our knees in front of GreedyGuts, who was wearing a dress made out of gummi bears. Savagely, she tore off bits of her dress and ate them while she berated us.

"Didn't I send you two on a PICNIC?"

A woman who looked like a llama pushed in. "Children these days are so ungrateful and selfish."

"I don't know why we have children," said a man who looked like a snake.

"You were all children once!" I said. The grown-ups were furious. Like I'd said a bad word.

"We were well-behaved children!" said the llama lady.

"Children, my nose!" said GreedyGuts. "These two won't be children for much longer."

"This is Dad's house, not yours!" said Hansel.

A woman wearing a shiny brown dress that said EAT ME waddled over. She looked like a human being made out of a bar of chocolate. GuzzleGuts.

"Who are YOU?" she said, dripping chocolate venom.

"His name's Handset," said GreedyGuts. "You see what I

have to put up with? All I wanted was for these children to starve to death while I had a little party."

The human chocolate bar shook her head, and thousands of little chocolate drops swished through the air.

"Look how you've upset Gutty!" she said. "After all she's done for you! Ignorant and shellfish—I mean selfish. BOGFACE! Get over here! If you want to be my boyfriend—do something!"

BogFace grabbed Hansel and threw him over one shoulder. I started kicking BogFace, but he just clamped his other hand around my neck and marched us off to his motorbike and sidecar.

"Get in or die!"

"My hero!" said GuzzleGuts, and she broke off a big piece of her chocolate dress and crammed it in his sweaty mouth.

BogFace straddled the bike, goggles and helmet on. Snatcher jumped up behind him. As we tore past the Little Tree, I reached out just in time, grabbed a branch, and then we were all flying down the road toward the city.

This time the journey was shorter. I watched the lights of the shops and the streetlights whizzing past us until BogFace screeched to a halt and Snatcher went flying off the back of the bike. He landed on all four feet, though, as cats always do.

We were at a gas station.

"This will do," said BogFace. "Now go and get a job, and don't come back till you've made a million dollars." He wheeled around on his motorcycle and was gone.

The city was so much bigger than the forest and so much more frightening. Nobody seemed to care that two children and a cat and a little tree were wandering through the streets late at night.

"Now we're in a pickle," said the Little Tree.

"A pickle would be great," I said. "I'm so hungry."

"There's a park over there," said Hansel. "Maybe those trees will know what to do."

We tried to cross the road once. We tried to cross the road twice. But the Little Tree was too slow.

"Lean me up by this lamppost. But don't forget to come back!"

So Hansel, Snatcher, and I ran as fast as we could across the busy road and into the dark of the park.

"Trees! Trees! Help us, please!" called Hansel.

"Hansel! Hansel!" said the trees. "We are lost too. We dream of the forest where we can never return."

"Ah," said a voice, "we are all lost, looking for the way home."

Sitting on a bench underneath an enormous umbrella was a very strange lady. She had a pointy nose, lots of black hair, only two teeth, and her eyes were red.

"Sit on either side of me," she said, "and you won't get wet." She asked us what we were doing out so late at night, and we told her about GreedyGuts, BeardFace, the forest, and everything else.

"You had better come home with me tonight," she said. "But a word of warning: don't eat my house."

Hansel made a face at me, meaning, *She's a weirdo, but what can you do, when you're lost and alone at night?*

The weirdo-woman got up to go, but Hansel said, "Our friend is waiting for us across the road—can we go there first, please?"

And we crossed the road. And the Little Tree waved its branches, and then, like when you catch a ball, and then, like when you know you're coming home, the weirdo-woman saw the Little Tree, and the Little Tree saw her, and in a minute, and in a second, they were dancing in each other's arms, and then we knew that this had to be the Witch in the Woods.

We passed through an empty parking lot into the late-night deserted space of a brightly lit shopping mall. The witch had a security tag that she held up against a metal gate. Suddenly we were inside a compound, with a big sign that said: GINGERBREAD HOUSE. TICKET HOLDERS ONLY.

The Gingerbread House was a little cottage with four windows and a front door. The door was a block of white chocolate. The gingerbread walls were a lovely pale brown color that gave off the most delicious smell, like cakes cooking. The windows were made of pretty colors of spun sugar. The chimney pots were little towers of whipped cream. In front of the house, under a little candy-stripe bridge, flowed a stream made of bubbling milk chocolate.

"Oh! Wow!" said Hansel, bending down and dipping in his finger. Quick as a mouse the witch grabbed his hand and licked off the chocolate.

"Oh! Gross!" said Hansel.

"One lick and you are doomed!"

We went inside. The chairs were made of nougat. The table was made of brown toffee. There was a neat little bed with edible pink flossy sheets. The cupboards overflowed with chocolate bars

and soda cans. My mouth was watering.

The witch reached inside a little fridge and gave us both a banana. I was a bit disappointed.

She said, "What you see here—this isn't normal sugar and normal chocolate and normal cake. It's a special recipe—and when you eat it, all you want is to eat more and more and more!"

Hansel and I looked at each other. *Should we trust her? Or was she crazy?*

She seemed to read our thoughts. "What am I? I'm just a straightforward, old-fashioned witch. I used to live in the wood where you found my dear friend the Little Tree. Back in those days I had magic apples, of course. Just like Snow White."

"That was an evil apple," I said.

"Well, yes, bad example. But magic fruit is fun."

The Little Tree said, "And then the bulldozers came . . ."

"Yes," said the witch sadly, "the bulldozers came."

"But why didn't you just turn them all into toads? Or magic yourself a new house?"

"Then they would've known that I have magic powers—and you don't want bad people to know about magic . . ."

"Absolutely not!" said the Little Tree. "Quite improper."

"He learned his English from a 1950s book of fairy tales," said the witch. "The logging company gave me a nasty little apartment in the city. There were no trees. I hated it—and that's when GuzzleGuts came to see me and offered me a deal."

"GuzzleGuts!"

"Yes. She promised me my very own Gingerbread House. She didn't say it would be in a shopping mall, or that I would have to wear a pointy hat and sharp teeth . . ."

"Why do you have to wear a pointy hat and sharp teeth?'

"It's like a Santa's Workshop thing. Kids come to see the wicked witch. I'm not wicked. But the house is wicked. It's made of Evil Gingerbread . . ."

"What's Evil Gingerbread?"

"When you eat it you never want to eat anything else—not real food like spaghetti Bolognese or baked potatoes or boiled eggs or fish and chips or grilled cheese. All you want to eat is Evil Gingerbread—and then GuzzleGuts sells it on her website. She gets rich, and the kids get sick."

"GuzzleGuts is best friends with GreedyGuts," I said.

"And GreedyGuts ate my blackbird," said Hansel.

"That's very bad," said the witch.

"Plus, we've lost our dad."

The witch got out her crystal ball, and we all held hands and thought about Dad. Suddenly a picture of him appeared. He looked thin and tired, stacking shelves in an empty supermarket.

"We have to rescue him!"

"And get our house back!"

"Fine," said the witch. "Are you scared of heights?"

The witch took us through the Gingerbread House to a little lock-up storage unit at the back. Inside there were two upright vacuum cleaners.

"Don't you have a broomstick?"

"Yes, of course I do, but it's vintage now. These go much faster." The witch pushed them out, and muttered something, and straight away the motors roared into life.

"Get on! Both of you on the red one— it's a bit of a squash, but you'll manage. I'll magnetize it to follow me. Hup, Snatcher! Hup, Little Tree!" said the witch, somehow balancing a tree on a vacuum cleaner high above the city.

The city looked like a string of lights. The city was yellow and

red. The cars were tiny mice, nose to tail. The city was empty of people in the deep, dark night, but not quite empty. A lone figure was leaving the back of the supermarket. His hands were in his pockets, his head held down.

"DAD! DAD!" we yelled like crazy.

Dad looked up. Were those his children traveling by vacuum cleaner?

"No time for a reunion right now!" shouted the witch, as she swooped to grab Dad by his belt.

"Pleased to meet you, Mr. Dad!" said the witch. "Here, hold this tree."

"Don't worry, Dad! We're going home!"

Soon we had crossed the city, and we were flying toward the woods.

Deep in the woods.
Deep in the woods.
Deep in the woods.

There's our house!

The party was over. Everyone had gone to bed. We landed

quietly. Dad got off, looking seasick, but the witch had been explaining things as we traveled, and Dad was furious about what GreedyGuts had done to us.

"Now listen," said the witch, "we need a plan. Everybody ready?"

The witch took out a bag and a paintbrush and painted our faces luminous orange. Now we glowed in the dark. Next she fixed pairs of bat wings onto Dad and Hansel, and gave me a big scary wig with eyes in the top.

"Now Greta—you and Hansel ride the vacuum cleaner and fly around the bedroom windows and rattle them until somebody wakes up. Then scare the daylights out of them! I'll find the GutGirls and deal with them.

"Mr Dad! Take this special green powder and throw it over BeardFace and BogFace. Are we all ready?"

The witch zoomed off. Dad quietly let himself in through the front door. Hansel and I switched on the vacuum cleaner and went straight up in the air till we were outside our bedroom window.

BANG! BANG! BANG!

"Who's that?" said a sleepy voice. PAD PAD PAD to the window.

"ARRGH! ARRGH! ARRGH!"

Crash! Down the stairs went Superman Pajamas, running for his life—because pajamas are not a superpower, and he couldn't fly.

Hansel and I were laughing so hard we nearly fell off the vacuum cleaner.

I steered downward, toward the front door. Out came BeardFace and BogFace, chased by Dad!

They saw me hovering on the vacuum cleaner with my glowing orange face and screamed, and then they looked at each other and screamed some more. The green powder Dad was throwing all over them was turning them into frogs. Froggy hands. Froggy feet. And

they were shrinking down down down, until all they could do was hop away, doing froggy croaking.

There was a fearsome shriek. Around the corner, riding her vacuum cleaner, came the witch, dragging GreedyGuts by her hair.

"What shall we do with her?"

"Put her in the pizza oven!" yelled Hansel.

"No! Wait! She's family!" said Dad. "We can't just put her in the pizza oven!"

"She's not family!" said the witch. "She's an ogre! Can't you tell?"

"I told you she was an ogre!" I said.

"Shove her in the pizza oven!" said Hansel again.

"Mercy, Mercy, Mercy!" wept GreedyGuts. "Dear children . . ." She turned to me. "Dear Gretna Green . . ."

"My name is Greta," I said. "Gretna Green is a place in Scotland."

"Such a clever girl," snivelled GreedyGuts. "And your brother, Hand Sanitiser. I mean, Handsome."

"He's Hansel. I'm Greta . . ."

GreedyGuts was sobbing on the floor in the remains of her gummi bear dress. Most of it had been eaten.

"I'll give you money!" (Wail, Wah, Wail.)

"All the money you stole from me?"

"Much more! Here's my life savings!" And she pulled out a big wad of cash from inside her underwear.

"Oh, yuck," said Hansel.

"Oh, woe!" wept GreedyGuts.

"Stop crying!" said the witch. "The only thing worse than an evil ogre is a crying ogre. Where's the other one?"

"Guzzi's dead!" said GreedyGuts. "Dead, Dead, Dead! She was pulling off her chocolate dress at bedtime, and it melted over her mouth and nose. She suffocated. I meant to call the ambulance, but I fell asleep . . . Oh, woe!"

"Oh, shut up!" said the witch. "I'll give you five minutes to run away. After that I set fire to your gummi bears."

With that, GreedyGuts hobbled off and was never seen again.

"Well, then . . ." said the witch. "All good. One last thing . . ."

The witch fumbled inside her mouth and pulled out her joke-shop teeth. Then she bent down and dislodged the red contact lenses she wore. Then she let loose her hair, took off her black cloak—and there she was in jeans and a T-shirt, with a big smile and hazel eyes.

"Greetings, Hansel and Greta! My name is Ruby, and you have freed me from a spell."

"What spell?"

"My own spell! The ones you cast on yourself are the really scary ones. I believed I had no power left. Just a life of Evil Gingerbread."

The Little Tree came hopping over.

"It is rather splendid to be free—but for me, freedom is staying in one place forever. Will somebody plant me, please?"

"I'll plant you," said Hansel.

"And I'll water you," I said.

Dad couldn't stop looking at Ruby. She was shining like a star, but that was the light inside her.

Dad said, "Ruby, you saved my children. That place called Gretna Green is a place where anybody can get married right away. We could get on the vacuum cleaner and go there right now!"

"You're not so bad, Mr. Dad, but we have to get to know each other first," said Ruby. "And see how the children feel about it all. So for now, shall we settle for a mug of hot chocolate?"

And straight through the air came four steaming mugs of hot chocolate, a saucer of milk for Snatcher, and a bag of compost for the Little Tree.

"Yes, I still have a bit of magic about me," said Ruby.

Dad and Ruby and Hansel and Greta, not forgetting Snatcher the cat, planted the Little Tree in their orchard, and bees came, and owls came, and deer came, and the air was full of birdsong.

And they all—yes, they all—lived
HAP HAPP HAPPILY.
Ever.
After.

AFTERWORD

At the heart of one story is another.

Fairy tales are like their own forests: hidden paths, twists and turns, bigger than they look, resistant to mapping.

These were stories told mouth by mouth, long before they were written down, but even in the writing they shot away, appearing again in a different place and time, recognizable but new.

"Hansel and Gretel" follows the well-known route of danger at home, exodus into the unknown, a place of safety that turns out to be perilous. Negative, wily female figures, positive, clever children, and help from the natural world.

I wanted to redeem the witch, but I didn't want to lose the ominous threat of the negative female in her greedy and controling aspect—a strong trope present in both the stepmother and the witch in the original story—and, interestingly, in Gretel herself, as she scoffs at the gingerbread house. Greed on the loose is—literally—all-consuming.

And that seemed like a good point of departure for my story. We live in a greedy society. We call ourselves consumers. Our guzzling selves are a real threat to each other and the planet. Bringing that in as a major theme naturally made me think about the valiant Greta Thunberg—a brave child, entirely suited to a fairy tale.

I wanted my version of the story to be funny. I like pantomime jokes and larger-than-life silliness. Above all, I like language, and there are such opportunities for language play in a good story with proper villains.

Speaking personally, I live in a wood. I was brought up by a non-related, physically large female of brooding aspect. I am small. I ran away. Animals and good luck have been on my side. I like gingerbread. I like a happy ending—as long as we remember that "hap" means fatefulness. And fate favors a true heart.

First published by Vintage Classics in 2020
This edition published by Haymarket Books in Chicago in 2021.
P.O. Box 180165
Chicago, IL 60618
773-583-7884
www.haymarketbooks.org
info@haymarketbooks.org

A CIP catalogue record for this book is available

ISBN: 978-1-64259-576-5

Distributed to the trade in the US through Consortium Book Sales and
Distribution (www.cbsd.com) and internationally through Ingram Publish-
er Services International (www.ingramcontent.com).

This book was published with the generous support of Lannan
Foundation and the Wallace Action Fund.

Special discounts are available for bulk purchases by organizations and
institutions. Please email info@haymarketbooks.org for more information.

Typeset and design by Friederike Huber

Printed in Canada.

2 4 6 8 10 9 7 5 3 1